D0568918

WHAT'S THE DIFFERENCE?

WHAT'S THE DIFFERENCE?

By DOYIN RICHARDS

Feiwel and Friends
NEW YORK

A Feiwel and Friends Book

An imprint of Macmillan Publishing Group, LLC.

Printed in the United States of America by Worzalla, Stevens Point, Wisconsin.
For information, address Feiwel and Friends, 175 Fifth Avenue, New York, N.Y. 10010.

Our books may be purchased in bulk for promotional, educational, or business use.
Please contact your local bookseller or the Macmillan Corporate and Premium Sales Department
at (800) 221-7945 ext. 5442 or by e-mail at MacmillanSpecialMarkets@macmillan.com.

Library of Congress Cataloging-in-Publication Data is available.

ISBN 978-1-250-10709-1

Book design by Rebecca Syracuse

Feiwel and Friends logo designed by Filomena Tuosto

First Edition—2017

The photos in this book were gathered by the author from his followers on Instagram and are used with permission.

10 9 8 7 6 5 4 3 2

mackids.com

My dad, Femi Richards, was raised in Sierra Leone and my mom, Laura, in the Deep South of Mississippi. Although their upbringings are vastly different, they shared the experience of witnessing unspeakable racism and discrimination firsthand while very young.

Although my parents easily could have harbored anger and bitterness as adults, they instead focused their energies on love, acceptance, and inclusion. They taught my two brothers and me that skin color, religion, sexual preference, socioeconomic status, etc., should never prevent us from being someone's friend. Now as dads, we're able to pass those messages down to our children.

It's a pretty simple path. Hate is a by-product of fear, and fear is a by-product of ignorance. In order to make the world a better place, we need to educate our children about how beautiful diversity truly is. *What's the Difference?* is a powerful tool to help.

I'm honored to dedicate this book to my mom and dad. They say you can't pick your parents, and that's why I thank my lucky stars every day that they were the ones who raised me.

TAKE A LOOK
AT YOURSELF.
Your friends may
not look like you,
and that's a
good thing.

WHAT'S THE DIFFERENCE if your friend has straight hair and yours is curly? All that matters is you love putting your hair inside funky hats together. And you do it in style.

WHAT'S THE DIFFERENCE if your neighbor has blue eyes and yours are brown? All that matters is when your eyes see ice cream, you eat it together.

WHAT'S THE DIFFERENCE

if your classmate has light skin and yours is a little darker?

All that matters is the artwork you create *TOGETHER* is as colorful as possible.

You see, little one, you
may not be the same on
the OUTSIDE as your
friends, but it's what
makes you different that
makes you *WONDERFUL*.

Don't be COLOR-BLIND.
The sky is blue during the day and black at night. If colors could talk, they would tell different stories about what they see when it's their turn to LIGHT UP THE WORLD.

It's the same with your friends.
LISTEN TO THEIR STORIES.

Because understanding your DIFFERENCES will create an unbreakable bond as you do the stuff you LOVE.

So play together.

Laugh together.

Get dirty together.

Get in trouble together.

And save the
world together.

The world *needs* you, little one.

I'm counting on you to set the example for grown-ups to follow.

Buy Me Some
Zoe
Zookeeper
Zookeeper
Bailey

Because when it comes to **LOVE**, keep showing that there really is no difference. It's all **AMAZING**. Just like you.